Dedicated with love to our children,
Noah, Immy, Zoe, Ben, Sam, Jed, Evie and Lucy,
and to the happy memories of seaside holidays we've
shared. You make us see things in a new way every day.

Tom was poorly. Tom was sad.

Tom was missing mummy and daddy.

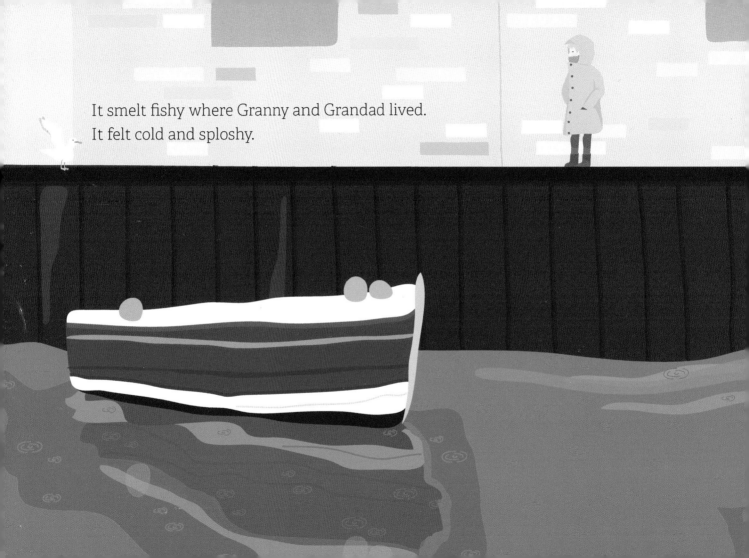

It smelt fishy where Granny and Grandad lived.
It felt cold and sploshy.

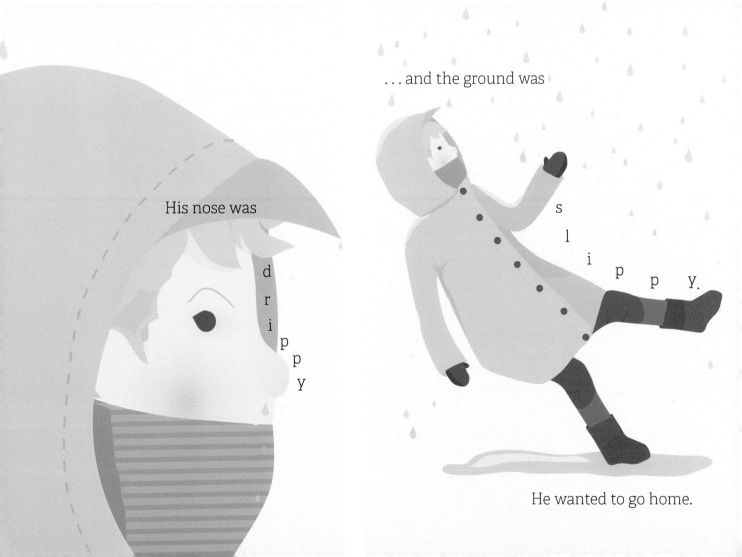

His nose was

d
r
i
p
p
y

. . . and the ground was

s
l
i
p
p y.

He wanted to go home.

Granny and Grandad tried to cheer him up.

But nothing

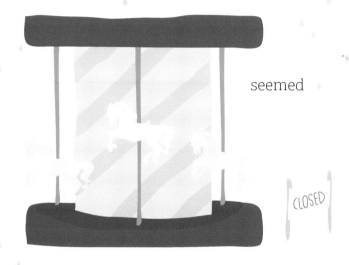

seemed

CLOSED

to work.

Grandad didn't like seeing Tom so glum.
"I've got just the thing to cheer you up . . ."

"Let's take the tram all the way to the top."

But Tom didn't want to go up there.

Tom covered his ears as the tram lurched up and up and up.

He wouldn't open his eyes.

Not even a blink.

Not even a crack.

And he certainly didn't want to catch the tram back down.

'I want to come home!" Tom cried.

Tom was feeling a bit better the next day.
"Let's try the tram again, Tom, all the way to the top."

His tummy twirled as the tram shuddered off.

He was so busy looking out he didn't notice the . . .

LUNK

SHUNT

WHIRR.

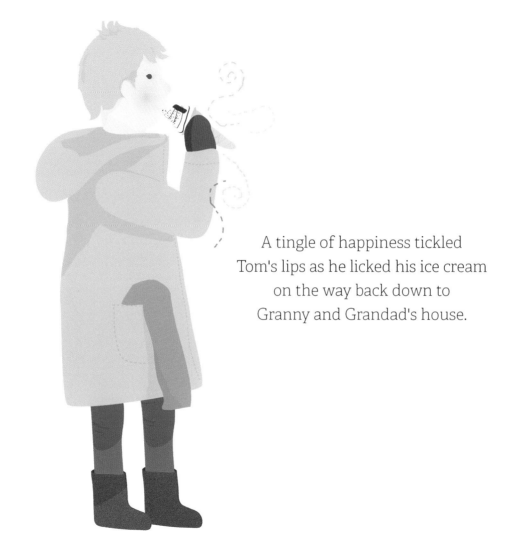

A tingle of happiness tickled
Tom's lips as he licked his ice cream
on the way back down to
Granny and Grandad's house.

If only he could tell his
mummy and daddy.

I went on the Tram ~~again~~ again today.

The people were tinyants *

I was tall TOM the giant

xxx

Mummy and Daddy

Central Tramway Company

Affix
stamp
here

Tom had a wonderful salty sleep that night.

But Grandad was still snoring
when Tom woke up.

At last . . .
"Can we take the
tram, Grandad,
all the way to
the top?"

Tom was the tram's first passenger today, rushing to get the best view, clutching his camera.

They were off.

Tom snapped busily on his camera.
Grandad smiled next to him.

SNAP

SNAP

SNAP

NAP

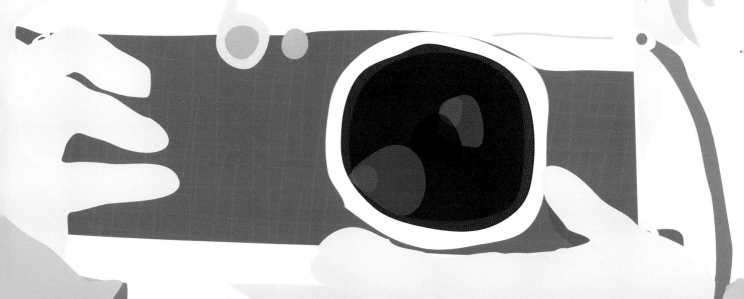

Grandad

Spade

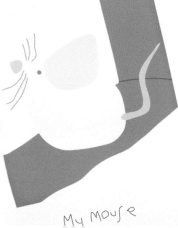

The tram place

My Mouse

me holding the tram

my ticket

BORO COUNCIL
CENTRAL TRAMWAY

CLIFF LIFT
SINGLE
UP

CHARGES DISPLAYED
AT POINT OF SALE

8011018

8011018

birds

Selfie

The best surprise was waiting for Tom at the top.

He couldn't wait to tell Mummy and Daddy all about his trips on the tram.

And that is just what he did.

The end . . .

. . . until Tom's next trip!

Me and Grandad
1978

Me and Grandad
2016

About Heritage Trams

Tom's tram is one of the 176 Heritage Railways and Tramways
around the UK. To find out more about these locations
go to www.heritagerailways.com.
You can visit Tom's tram in Scarborough, North Yorkshire,
near the Grand Hotel. Built in 1881 it has carried lots of boys
and girls with their families over the years.
Discover more about the Tramway at
www.centraltramway.co.uk.

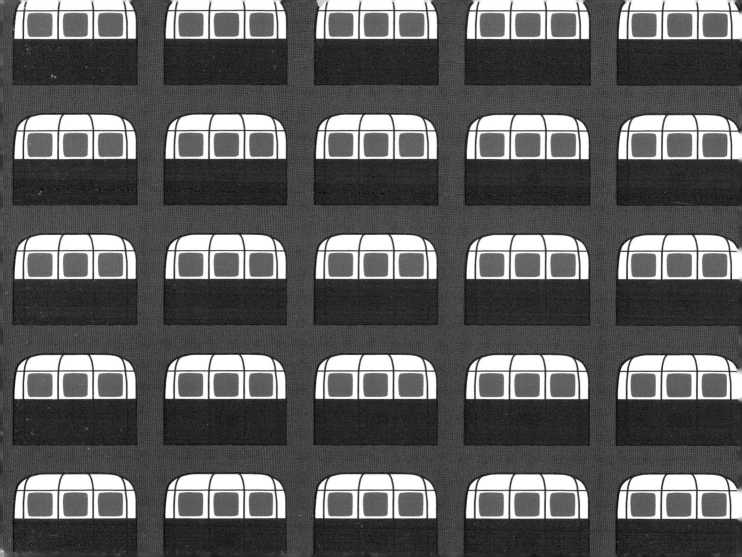